THE EYEBROWS OF DOOM

Steve Smallman   Miguel Ordóñez

tiger tales

In the woods in a cave, a big bear named Dave
was sweeping his floor with a broom,
when two clumps of hair leaped into the air

and cried,

To our beautiful Annie (who likes weird stuff!)

— S. S.

A Miquel, Julen, Zuri y Joan. Familia amiga.

— M. O.

tiger tales
5 River Road, Suite 128, Wilton, CT 06897
Published in the United States 2022
Originally published in Great Britain 2022
by Little Tiger Press Ltd.
Text copyright © 2022 Steve Smallman
Illustrations copyright © 2022 Migel Ordóñez
ISBN-13: 978-1-68010-267-3
ISBN-10: 1-68010-267-2
Printed in China
LTP/2800/4069/0921
10 9 8 7 6 5 4 3 2 1

www.tigertalesbooks.com

"No, you're not!

You're two slugs
all covered in hair."

But they laughed,

WE'LL SHOW **YOU**
WHAT TWO EYEBROWS
CAN DO!

And

just

look

what

they

did

to

the

bear!

Poor Dave felt so strange —

everything seemed to change

as the
eyebrows
took over
his mind.

And try as he might,

he just couldn't fight

the urge to do something UNKIND.

Some campers nearby saw the look in Dave's eye
as he ran up and crashed through the fence.

Dave ate all of their food,
which was terribly rude,

then he jumped up and
down on their tents!

The eyebrows pounced on
a young seagull named Ron,

who shot
into the air
with a whoop.

He flew over the bay,
then he squawked,

"Bombs away!"

and he pelted
the people
with POOP!

MORE FUN,
EYEBROW ONE?

CAN DO,
EYEBROW TWO!

Little Molly, all wriggly, and gurgly, and giggly, looked incredibly sweet until . . .

WOWZERS!

With a mischievous scream,
she smeared her ice cream
on the back of her grandfather's trousers!

All was peaceful and still in the zoo on the hill,

until in crept the　　　　　　　two eyebrow pests.

They hopped on the head
of poor Porcupine Ned,

and he ran around poking the guests!

Then a rhino named Rover
knocked the garbage cans over.

Sue Skunk made
a terrible smell.

A hippo named Bud
showered people with mud,

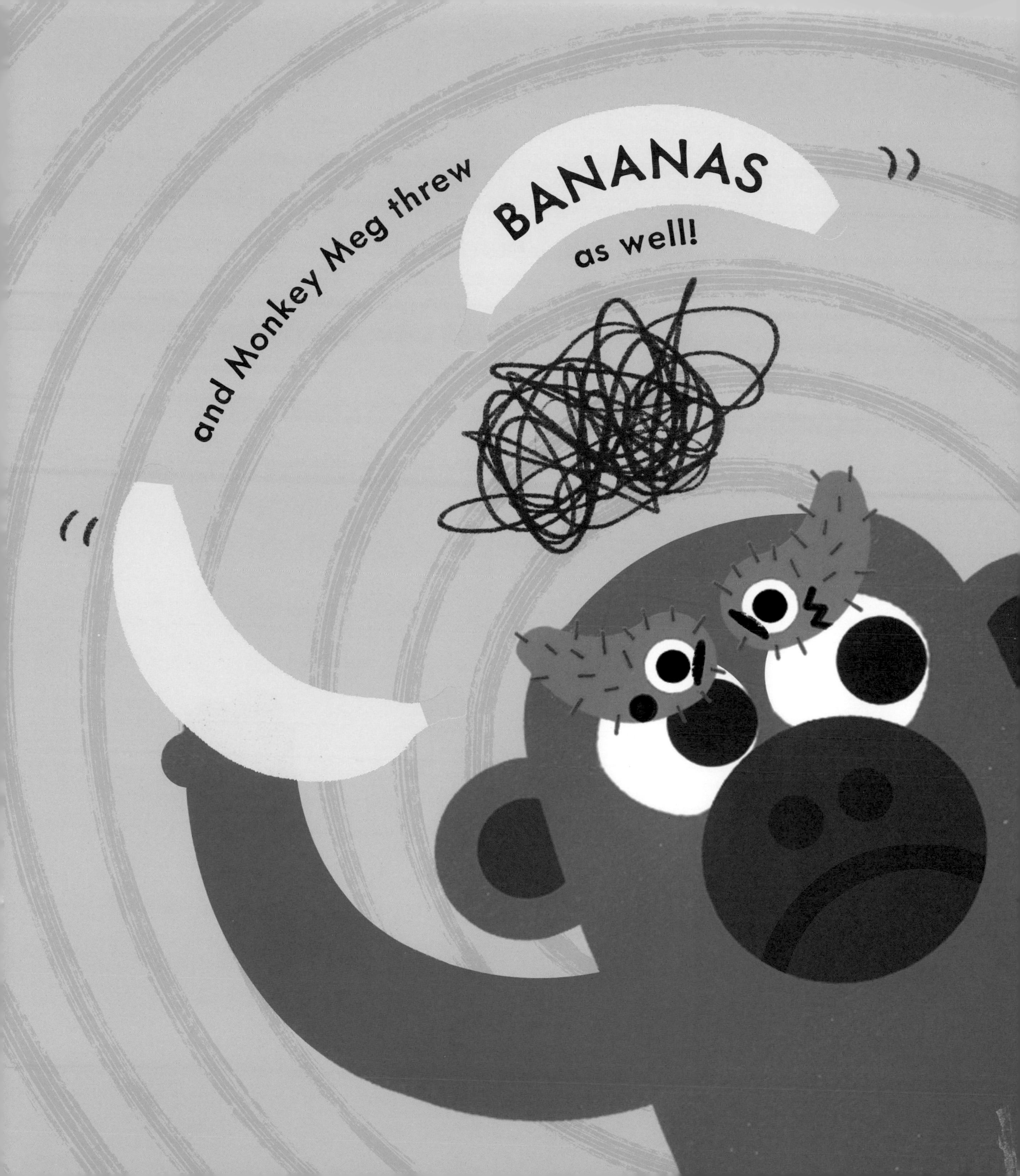
and Monkey Meg threw
BANANAS
as well!

The zookeeper, John, shouted,

"What's going on?
You've never been like this before!"

Dave ran in with his broom.
"It's the Eyebrows of Doom!

They're scuttling
around on the floor!"

So Brow One and Brow Two

ran all over the zoo,

trying hard to find

ZOO

somewhere to hide.

In a panic they chose
Edna Elephant's nose,

and they rapidly wiggled inside!

Edna Elephant's eyes
opened wide with surprise;

she hiccuped and sneezed, then . . .

KABOOM!

Out like a shot,

all covered in snot,

flew the terrible Eyebrows of Doom!

They splashed into the sea,
and the crowd cheered, "Yippeeeeeee!
Let's get back to our nice afternoon."

"We're safe now!"
squawked Ron.

"THE
EYEBROWS
ARE
GONE!"

But he just might have spoken too soon!